Tommy at the Grocery Store

Tommy at the Grocery Store

by Bill Grossman
illustrated by Victoria Chess

Harper & Row, Publishers

TOMMY AT THE GROCERY STORE

Typography by Carol Barr
10 9 8 7 6 5 4 3 2 1
First Edition

Library of Congress Cataloging-in-Publication Data
Grossman, Bill.
Tommy at the grocery store.

Summary: Tommy is mistaken for items in a grocery
store until his mother comes to the rescue.
[1. Grocery trade—Fiction.   2. Shopping—Fiction.
3. Stories in rhyme]   I. Chess. Victoria, ill.
II. Title.
PZ8.3.G914To   1989   [E]   88-35756
ISBN 0-06-022408-8
ISBN 0-06-022409-6 (lib. bdg.)

To Donna, Josh, Adam, and Sally

B.G.

To Claire Clifton

V.C.

Tommy's mommy left poor Tommy

Sitting at the grocery store.

The grocer found poor Tommy sitting,

Playing on the grocery floor.

He thought that Tommy was salami

And set him on the deli shelf.

And Tommy sat among salamis,

Softly sobbing to himself.

A housewife came and bought poor Tommy,

Thinking he was meat,

And put him in a shopping bag

And took him home to eat.

She was just about to slice him
When she shouted with surprise,
"Oh, my goodness! Gracious! Dear!
My salami! It has eyes!

"This is not salami,"

Said the housewife, looking closer.

"It's a potato; it has eyes."

And she took him to the grocer.

"Take this back!" she shouted.

And the grocer took him back

And put him with potatoes

In a brown potato sack.

Pretty soon a doctor came

And purchased the potatoes

And stuffed poor Tommy in a basket

With pickles and tomatoes.

She was just about to cook him

When she shouted, "Holy heck!

Sakes alive! My goodness!

This potato has a neck!

"This isn't a potato,"

Said the doctor, looking closer.

"It's a bottle; it has a neck."

And she took him to the grocer.

"Take this bottle back," she said.

And the grocer took him back

And put him with the bottles

On a soda bottle rack.

A construction worker bought him

And was walking out the door

When he shouted, "Hey, there's skin here

On this bottle from the store!

"This is not a bottle,"

Said the worker, looking closer.

"It's a banana; it has skin."

And he took him to the grocer.

"Take this back!" he hollered.

And the grocer took him back

And put him with bananas

On a big banana stack.

Next a teacher bought him
And took him home to eat
And very nearly fainted
When she noticed he had feet.

"This isn't a banana,"

Said the teacher, looking closer.

"It's a ruler; it has feet."

And she took him to the grocer.

"Take this ruler back," she said.

And the grocer took him back

And put him with the rulers

In a yellow ruler pack.

An artist lifted up the rulers

And shouted, "Oh, my dear!

Goodness gracious! My, oh my!

This ruler has an ear!

"This is not a ruler,"

Said the artist, looking closer.

"It is corn; it has ears."

And he took him to the grocer.

So Tommy sat among the corncobs,

Looking quite forlorn,

Until a postman came and bought him,

Thinking he was corn.

He put him in his mail truck
In a bag with other corn,
But Tommy reached out with his leg
And beeped the postman's horn.

"That surely isn't corn in there,"
Said the postman, looking closer.
"It's a table; it has legs."
And he took him to the grocer.

"No, that's not a table,"
Said the grocer with alarm.
"Mister, that's a chair you're holding.
See, it has an arm.

"Set it down," the grocer said.

"I'd like to sit awhile."

Suddenly a pretty lady

Scurried up the aisle.

She took poor Tommy in her arms
And hugged his little head.
"You're much too warm and much too sweet
To be a chair," she said.

"Warm and sweet," the grocer said.

"Lady, that's a pie."

"If that's a pie," the lady said,

"Then, Mister, so am I."

"Mommy! Mommy! It's my mommy!"

Shouted Tommy, hugging closer.

And she held his hand and took him home.

"Thank goodness," said the grocer.

JP
Grossman, Bill.
Tommy at the grocery store
$12.95

DATE DUE

FEB 27 '93	OCT 30 '96	JUN 0 2 2000
AUG 31 '93	NOV 20 '96	
NOV 5 '93	FEB 1 '97	FEB 24 2001
OCT 14 '94	MAY 17 '98	
MAY 10 '95	MAY 1 '98	
JUL 5 '95	MAY 26 '98	
AUG 8 '95	AUG 27 1999	
SEP 29 '95	APR 5 2000	